I0538723

"Destiny Is All I Need"

2ND EDITION

NOVEL BY

EBONY NICOLE

DESTINY IS ALL I NEED

DESTINY IS ALL I NEED

Copyright © 2014 Ebony Nicole

Printed in the United States

ISBN-13:978-0692354292
ISBN-10:0692354298

Printed by Createspace 2014
Revised and Re-published by BlaqRayn Publishing Plus 2014

Cover Design: ESTETIKA EXPOSURE/A. Marie
Editor: Windy Goodloe

Ebony Nicole

PRESENTS:

DESTINY IS ALL I NEED
2ND EDITION

A Novel

Prologue

Sometimes, in relationships, we don't always know the right way to go, but, in my opinion, when one has made up her mind to do something, it's best to let it be. In the end, somebody always ends up getting hurt, but I'm choosing not to be the fool. In this case, I have to stay on top of it all.

When that bitch showed up at my door, all kinds of shit went through my head. Trying to be the bigger woman probably made me look like a damn fool in her eyes. The heart tends to beat to another tune when love is involved, but I wasn't ready to face the music. I listened to the lies, shed my silent tears. In the end, I am still a winner in my eyes. Destiny played all of her cards until she was down to the last one— me! Where was everybody else when she needed them to be there? We could have had it all together, just like old times. Love doesn't always give you what you want, but I guess she'd made her mind up at the end. I just wish things could have been different for us. Although my heart still loves Destiny, I'm nobody's fool.

Chapter 1

My Lady, My Wife

Ashley

"Baby, come here! I want to show you something! I've put everything in order for the awards program!"

When her lady walked into the living room, she almost forgot what she had called her for because she wanted to work on her instead. *Fuck a project*, she thought as she smiled at her girlfriend, admiring her sexy ass, pretty brown skin, dark brown eyes, and body to kill for. Her name was Destiny Phillips. They had met six years ago at a conference that had been held by Ashley's former employer.

Ashley Willington was now the thirty-year-old vice president of the Royalties. It had started out in 2010 and was a thriving business that concentrated on helping the youth. Now, the Royalties was doing big things, and it only kept getting better. The Royalties was a nationwide establishment that helped young adults become vice presidents, CEOs, and entrepreneurs. It provided them with the skills they needed to become successful in life.

"What is it that has you yelling my name at the top of your lungs, sexy?" Destiny asked.

When she saw the smile on Ashley's face, she knew Ashley had come up with yet another great idea. After she sat down next to Ashley, Destiny reached for Ashley's folder. Ashley didn't say anything as Destiny looked over her work. She wanted Destiny's honest opinion of it, which was what she always got anyway. That was the best part of having a better half— she was always there when she was needed.

"This is perfect, love. I can't wait to see it in effect. You've done so much for these young adults, and they appreciate the effort."

"Thank you, babe. I really do try to make sure they have what they need. I can't wait for the award ceremony. They are going to be so surprised," Ashley said in return.

Ashley had been working hard, on a daily basis, trying to make sure everything was set for the program. She took pride in her work because she knew it was a reflection of her. It was amazing how much she had changed over the years. She had never thought she would be in this position— Ms. CEO. She had a lot to be proud of.

Each day, when she came home from work, she could feel the hard work that she had put in throughout the day. Each program, meeting, or conference had to have her approval. All of the meetings and decision-making made her days seem long. Rarely did everything go perfectly, which left her with nothing to do, so, she would work on the special projects that she had created. Ashley wanted to make sure they were perfect.

Now that she was done with all of that, she could move on to even better things. Destiny, to be exact. After a long day at work, the only thing Ashley wanted to do was unwind. She put her work away and headed straight to the bathroom to freshen up. After seeing Destiny looking so damn good, making love was the only thing on her mind. Ashley came out of the bathroom, wrapped in a towel, her body still slightly damp from the shower.

When she walked into their bedroom, Destiny was sitting on the edge of the bed. Ashley slowly walked in front of her and dropped the towel. Destiny already knew what time it was, and she was ready. She quickly removed the clothes she had on and grabbed Ashley by her waist. She loved the softness of her skin. Destiny placed kisses on her stomach. Then, she stood up and gently laid Ashley down on the bed.

"Ah, Destiny! That's my spot, babe. Ooh, you make me feel so good," Ashley moaned a few minutes later.

Her girl was putting it down, and Ashley was embracing every minute of it. "Whose pussy is this, baby? Tell me it's mine," Destiny whispered.

At that moment, Ashley exploded all over Destiny's lips. The bed was soaking wet, just like her pussy. Her stomach tightened as Destiny continued to please her over and over. Destiny had the softest lips, and Ashley thought they felt lovely sucking on her. Just when she thought it was over, Destiny turned her over, onto her stomach, and licked her pussy from behind. Her fingers teased Ashley's clit. She couldn't believe how good she was feeling. Her body was doing things she didn't know it could!

"Um, baby, I'm cumming for you. You want me

to cum for you?"

Destiny was moaning, too, and Ashley knew Destiny was wet just from giving her pleasure. Ashley reached between Destiny's legs and felt how wet she was. Then, Ashley licked Destiny's juices. She loved when Ashley did that. The next position was 69 because Ashley wanted to give just as much pleasure as she had received. Destiny couldn't handle it as Ashley's tongue went to work on her. It felt so good. Destiny loved all the freaky shit Ashley did to her. She never left one inch of her body untouched. They were in the groove, just pleasing each other, like lovers do. They couldn't hear anything but the music that they are making.

After two hours, they were still going strong. They weren't going to stop until they heard: "Destiny! Destiny! Come out here! I know that you are in there, so come on outside!"

It was Crystal, yelling from the driveway. Ashley

and Destiny stopped and looked at each other. Then, they looked towards the window. They saw a vehicle parked in their driveway. Confused, Ashley got out of the bed and put her clothes on. She had to see who this bold bitch was, calling her fiance's name like that. Destiny moved quickly, throwing on some shorts and a wife beater. Ashley knew something was up by how quickly Destiny moved around their bedroom.

Destiny didn't want Ashley to go to the door, knowing Crystal was outside. It was really going to be some shit, and she wasn't ready for it.

"Wait, baby, wait! Don't go to the door. Let me handle it," Destiny said as she quickly got out of the bed.

"Handle what? What is going on?" Ashley asked.

"Nothing, baby! I swear! Just lie down, and I'll be right back. I promise."

"You got me fucked up! I'm going to see what the hell is going on!"

DESTINY IS ALL I NEED

Ashley was close on Destiny's heels as they made their way to the front door. Crystal was already halfway up the walkway by that time. This was the shit Destiny didn't want to face. This was the time for Destiny to put everything on the line. Her secret had showed up right at her doorstep.

Chapter 2

Crystal's Here

Destiny

"What the fuck is wrong with you, showing up at my house?" Destiny screamed.

"Whatever! I told you I wasn't going to play second to no bitch. I don't care if she is your fiance."

"Hold the fuck up! Who are you calling a bitch? I don't know who you are, but you got some nerve coming to my muthafuckin' house," Ashley yelled.

Ashley walked towards Crystal. Now, she was the bold one. Destiny's mind was working overtime as she thought of ways to diffuse this situation. She didn't understand how she had ended up with this crazy broad on her team.

"Watch your fucking mouth, Crystal!"

DESTINY IS ALL I NEED

As Ashley and Crystal stood toe to toe, Destiny tried to get in between them before shit got out of hand, but she was too late. Ashley was heated, and she wanted answers.

"I'm going to ask you one time and one time only. Who the fuck are you? I don't know what's going on, but you crossed the line when you showed up at my doorstep."

Crystal stood there, dumbfounded. The buck she had in her was gone. She wasn't mad at Ashley. Besides, she didn't even know her. Destiny was the one to blame. She was the one who had told her all of those lies, making her believe they were going to be together. All the blame should have been on her. Crystal didn't open her mouth. She was making herself look stupid.

"Ask Destiny why I'm here. This is all her fault," Crystal said as she turned around and walked back to her car. The tears that had welled up in her eyes fell freely as she got in and started the engine.

Ashley was stunned, but hurt was the best word to describe her. She wanted to lay hands on Destiny and this bitch that had mysteriously appeared at her house. But what would that solve? The battle wasn't with this chick; it was with Destiny.

After making her way past Destiny, Ashley went back into the house. She was more confused than she was before she'd come out.

Crystal pulled out of the driveway in a hurry. This was not how she had planned for this trip to go. Nothing had been confirmed but the obvious— Destiny had a woman, and it wasn't her. She sped out so fast that you would have thought the car was on two wheels.

After jumping on the highway, Crystal did ninety all the way. As she drove further away, her mind was still at Destiny's house. As she drove, more tears formed in her eyes. As she cried harder, her vision became blurry.

DESTINY IS ALL I NEED

She was barely able to see as she switched from lane to lane, acting like she was the only driver on the road. She hit the HOV lane, and opened it up, rolling with every curve of it. It seemed that she knew the curves well as she maneuvered her way through, but one was a little steep and, with the speed she was going, it caused her to lose control of the car. It did a complete 360 before hitting the wall. Then, another car sped up and hit her head on.

All around, horns blared as everybody else swerved, trying to avoid the accident. A couple of drivers pulled over to the side to see if they could help. One man stayed there and dialed 911. He and another driver were unable to move Crystal, so they had no choice but to wait for help. When the police arrived, they got all of the details from the male who had called. The ambulance arrived shortly after and attended to Crystal and the other injured driver. Crystal didn't want to go to the hospital;

all she wanted to do was go home. Her wishes were not granted as she was settled onto the gurney and hauled off to the hospital.

This shit is all Destiny's fault, she thought as her mind drifted back to the day that they had met. It was all good back then but like the saying goes, "All good things must come to an end".

*****

There she was having a good time. The woman she was with was beautiful— even Crystal had to admit that. They had drinks in their hands, and their attention was on each other. Every so often, they would look up to watch the dancers, but it was obvious that their conversation was more interesting. Anyway, Crystal saw her, and she knew she wanted her for herself. She was so fucking sexy that Crystal wished she was the chick in front of her who was getting all of her attention. Seeing

DESTINY IS ALL I NEED

this, she just played it cool, but, if she got the chance to approach, she was going to do just that.

Thirty minutes later, she was sitting alone, so Crystal walked up and said, "What's up?"

Crystal had to say it twice because the music blared from the speakers as everyone danced around in the club. The woman looked at her with the prettiest brown eyes that Crystal had ever seen. Crystal tried to strike up a conversation, but, by that time, the woman's companion was coming back, so Crystal quickly stepped to the side to make it appear as if she hadn't been at their table. The woman smiled as her woman took her seat. Crystal was disappointed, but she kept it moving, for the time being.

Once she was back at her table, she continued to watch her every move, and, to Crystal's surprise, the woman glanced her way every so often. Now, Crystal knew she had a chance...

DESTINY IS ALL I NEED

Chapter 3

Let Me Explain

Destiny

Destiny walked as fast as she could to catch up with Ashley. The only thing she was concerned with was trying to fix the mess she had made. Everything had been going according to plan until she stepped out of her relationship. For six years, she had been committed to loving Ashley, but temptation was a muthafucka, and she couldn't resist. If it was the last thing she did, she would explain everything to Ashley and make it right.

She was ready for whatever Ashley had in store for her, but, when they got in the house, Ashley went straight to their room and started packing her shit. There was no reason for her to stay, and Destiny couldn't explain the shit that had just gone down. It was best that they be apart for a while. Destiny sat down on the bed and tried to get Ashley to listen, but Ashley just kept throwing clothes in her overnight bag.

"Baby, please don't go! Give me a chance to explain. You can't just leave like this."

"Says who? I don't know what kind of games you are playing, but I'm not the one to play them with. You got some fucking nerve, having some bitch come to our house as if she is confronting me about *you!* You are supposed to be my woman, but I can't tell."

"Baby, it's not ..."

Destiny's words trailed off. There was really no need to explain. Ashley continued to move around the room, ignoring every word that came out of Destiny's mouth from that point on. When she was done packing her things, she walked out of the room to the front door and let it slam in Destiny's face. Destiny felt like a damn fool. What could she say now to get Ashley to come back home?

For now, all she could do was think. She and Ashley were the perfect couple. They did everything together; they were one. When you saw Destiny, there was Ashley and vice versa. Destiny loved her so much, and, now that she'd messed up, she could only hope that Ashley would come back to her. She was thirty-five years old now and had thought her "chasing women" days were over. That was until she saw Crystal at the club.

At first, she wasn't paying her any attention, until she left the table that Ashley and Destiny were sharing. She was cute, but she was not as beautiful as Ashley. Crystal was light-skinned with hazel eyes and had a cute little shape to be so slim. She was not Destiny's usual taste, but there was something about the way she had approached her. She knew she'd seen Ashley there, but she didn't care. Crystal knew what she wanted. That was what started it all.

DESTINY IS ALL I NEED

After that day, she saw her again at Bank of America. They conversed for a while, exchanged numbers, and promised to keep in touch. That was right after Ashley and Destiny had celebrated their five year anniversary...DAMN!

Destiny knew she should have stuck to her plan, which was to go out and just have a good time. That one night turned into one year, but now it had to be over. All kinds of thoughts were floating through her mind at that time. She couldn't concentrate on one thing because getting Ashley to come back was her number one mission. It was funny how the shit had played out.

Her phone rang, interrupting her thoughts. She hurried up and answered, hoping it was Ashley on the other end. To her surprise, Crystal's name appeared on the screen. She answered with an attitude.

"Hello!"

"Is this Destiny Phillips?" a male's voice asked.

"Yes. May I ask who I'm speaking with?"

"Ms. Phillips, my name is Dr. O'Conner, the family practitioner at Saving Lives Family Practice. I have a young lady here by the name of Crystal Simmons. She asked that we call you. She's been in a terrible car accident. She hit a wall doing ninety miles per hour. The car spun around and hit another car head on."

Destiny was at a loss for words as she listened with her head in her hands. She responded slowly.

"Uh, I'm sorry, Dr. O'Conner, but I don't know anybody by that name. Maybe, you dialed the wrong number."

Destiny didn't want to be on the phone and was doing her best to get off.

"Well, Ms. Simmons said—"

She quickly hung up her phone. She was not ready to address anything dealing with Crystal. She had other things to deal with. Even though Destiny knew she was probably the cause of whatever had happened to Crystal, she was not about to get involved.

Destiny felt terrible, but she would have to get over it. This only put more pressure on her than what she already had. Destiny never thought one night could turn her life upside down. Now, Crystal was in the hospital all because of her, and she couldn't be there. She had to take one step at a time to fix this bullshit.

Chapter 4

What's the Deal?

Ashley

While doing eighty miles per hour on I-285, Ashley's mind was racing. She didn't know what to think or how to feel. The only thing she remembered was seeing this bitch show up at her house. It seemed like her mind went blank after that. She wanted to relax a bit, so Ashley went to a hotel not far from their house. Hopefully, this was something that could be worked out. They had never had any major issues in their relationship, but, if Destiny did not want her, why should she stay around?

After getting settled into her room, Ashley sat down on the bed and replayed the incident in her head. She wasn't a little girl anymore. She was indeed a

DESTINY IS ALL I NEED

grown-ass woman with no time for bullshit, but all of their lovemaking had messed up her mind.

Sometimes, when you are in love, your thoughts aren't clear until something major happens. That's when the smokes clear, opening up your eyes to the lies that you tried to ignore, Ashley thought.

She knew all that she had been through before Destiny came along. Since Ashley didn't want to get anywhere near that type of lifestyle again, she knew it would be best if she left, but Destiny had saved her from that hell hole she called a relationship. Coming into her life and turning it around had seemed so easy for her to do. Destiny respected her and loved her with everything she had.

As she thought about all the good times they'd shared, tears streamed down her face. Her heart was broken, and she felt so weak. Ashley wished she was in Destiny's arms at that moment, where she had always felt safe. She contemplated calling to see what the deal was, but she didn't see why she had to. Instead, she cried herself to sleep as she thought about happier times between her and Destiny.

When she woke up, Ashley checked the time on her phone, it was 4:30 A.M. She realized she had slept three hours away. She was happy to see that Destiny had been trying to contact her. Even though there were no voice-mails, Ashley decided to return the call. She was upset when Destiny's phone went straight to voice-mail.

Instead of calling back, Ashley got up, got dressed, and headed back to her house. She couldn't say how all of this would turn out, but she was sick of not knowing. Ashley was determined to get some answers because she believed she deserved the truth, even if it hurt her.

Chapter 5

I'm In So Much Pain

Crystal

Dr. O'Conner rushed into Crystal's room after hearing something crash to the floor. When he entered, the patient's food was scattered everywhere. That was a good sign, being that she had been laid up for almost three weeks, paralyzed from the waist down. Crystal wasn't aware of how bad the accident was or how bad her condition as a result of the accident because she had not been responding to anybody. Now that she was aware of her surroundings, she had plenty of questions.

"OMG! Where am I? Who are you? What happened?"

"Ma'am, please don't try to move. It would be best if you just lie still, okay?" Dr. O'Conner warned.

"I...I...I..."

"Ma'am, just keep still for me, and I'll explain everything to you."

He tried his best to make her comfortable again. Once she seemed to relax, he explained what had happened. He told her that she had been in a very bad car accident which had caused paralysis from the waist down.

Dr. O'Conner went on to say that it could be temporary if she allowed them to keep her in their care a little while longer. Crystal didn't seem understand anything that was being said to her. When she heard the word "paralysis", she screamed as loud as she could, completely forgetting the tubes running through her body. Screaming only causing her more pain as Dr. O'Conner tried to comfort her. He knew she was going through this alone.

His heart went out to her, and he felt like doing everything he could to help. When she calmed down a little, Dr. O'Conner had a nurse bring more food and drink to her room.

After picking at a little food from the tray and taking a few sips, she drifted back to sleep. She prayed when she woke up, she would be back at her home, in her own bed. Being with Destiny had been all she'd wanted for the past year. Now, it seemed like she had to find something else to occupy her time.

Despite her current situation, Crystal was still in love. Destiny was unaware, but she had been Crystal's first experience. At twenty-one, she hadn't had relations with men or women. She had run off all the males that had tried to approach her, but her curiosity about women was what had led her to the club that night. Females had always been interesting to her. She would flirt with them all the time. Through all of that, she was still a virgin. In her mind, Crystal hoped that everything would turn out in her favor.

DESTINY IS ALL I NEED

As she took a look at her surroundings, she wasn't so sure about that. On top of all this mess, her head was hurting. It felt like a ton of bricks were just sitting there, holding her head in one spot.

Chapter 6

I Fucked Up

Destiny

It was 5:00 A.M., and Destiny was still in shock from all the shit that was going on. She hadn't moved from the spot she was in for hours. She had attempted to call Ashley several times but didn't get an answer. She was so worried, and her head ached, but she decided to go look for Ashley as she got up from the floor.

As she walked towards the door, she heard the lock click and in walked Ashley. Her eyes were bloodshot from crying all night. Destiny froze, not knowing where to start explaining.

She walked over to Ashley, and they hugged each other; neither wanted to let go. Their eyes spoke as they gazed at one another. Destiny knew that she had to speak first because she did not want to waste any more time, so she told everything.

Ashley sat there, not knowing how to take it as she heard how Destiny and Crystal met, how they fucked around, went out to dinner, and, most importantly, made love on a regular. Many of the times that Destiny had been missing she was with Crystal.

It wasn't long before tears were in Ashley's eyes again. What she had thought wasn't true turned out to be. All the words that Destiny spoke after the confession, Ashley didn't hear. Her heart didn't want to feel any more pain. She couldn't even look Destiny in her eyes.

When Destiny was finished talking, she tried to console Ashley. She knew getting back on track was going to be a task, and that was only if Ashley was willing to try. On top of that, she had failed to tell Ashley about Crystal ending up in the hospital. She thought it would be too much for her to handle all in one day.

DESTINY IS ALL I NEED

Destiny figured that letting that part go would help her get over Crystal all together. Until that phone call, she hadn't realized how much she cared about Crystal. She knew that loving and being in love were two different things. When she and Crystal were with each other, they made love, but Destiny knew her heart belonged to Ashley.

Destiny couldn't take the silence, so she got up and headed to the bedroom. Once she was in the room, she closed the door and tried to pull herself together.

Exiting the room an hour later, she found Ashley coming through the door with her bags in her hands. Destiny rushed to her side because she realized that she was getting her things out of the car. In her mind, this was a sign that they could work through this.

Ashley looked at Destiny and simply said, "I'm giving you a chance to fix this, but don't think, for one minute that because I'm in love with you, I won't leave your ass. Whatever loose ends need to be tied, I suggest you to do so and quickly."

Destiny was shocked beyond words. All she could say was, "Okay, baby. I love you so much."

"I love you, too."

They hugged again, but, this time, it ended with a kiss. This still didn't help Ashley feel better, but they did have time under their belt. She wasn't the type to just walk away. Although her mind was telling her to leave, her heart wouldn't let her go. She loved Destiny more than anything, and she didn't want their relationship to end like this. Maybe, with time, they would get back to the way they used to be. Destiny had lost some of Ashley's trust, though. That was for sure.

No one was dumb enough to put all of their trust in a relationship that had been damaged. Ashley had done nothing to deserve this, but here she was, giving it another try.

DESTINY IS ALL I NEED

Chapter 7

The Big Event

Ashley

It was time for the 2009 Awards Ceremony! Ashley was so excited about it. She hoped everything went as she had planned it.

For starters, she was dressed to kill. The black dress she wore caressed and showcased her curves and flawless skin, and her heels gave her short frame a little more height. Ashley knew she looked sexy, and Destiny, who was right beside her, looked equally as sexy. She was stylin' in her two-piece pant suit.

In Ashley's presence, Destiny felt very relaxed, more like herself. Together, they turned heads throughout the ceremony. As Ashley looked around, she was delighted to see all the people that she worked with on a daily basis were able to attend. Everybody was excited and looking good for the occasion.

The room was decorated nicely with gold and black decor. Everything was nicely set up. Sitting at a table in the middle of the floor were the young adults that Ashley loved so much. That evening was theirs, and she wanted it to be perfect. Ashley walked around and introduced Destiny to everybody. Now, it was time to be seated and give out awards. That was Ashley's favorite part because it showed everybody the progress of these young adults and it let them know how important they were and that they could do whatever they wanted to.

Ashley took her place at the podium and welcomed everybody to the ceremony. Then, she called all of her crew's names, one at a time. They were all happy as they received awards for different accomplishments. It really surprised them because they didn't know that the whole event was for them. Ashley had made sure everybody played along, and it turned out to be just what she had expected.

Chapter 8

I Need to Go Home

Crystal

Frantically, Crystal looked around her hospital room after she woke up in a cold sweat. When she realized that she wasn't at home in her own bed, she started to cry. She had been in the hospital for almost a month now, and she missed Destiny.

Often, she wondered why she hadn't been to see her. Maybe, it really was over. There was so much she wanted to do outside these doors. She was tired of sleeping and crying since that was all she seemed to do lately. All of her daily activities were on hold, and she couldn't adapt to it. Just when her life was getting in order, this happened. She would only think these things because she did not want to seem ungrateful.

Crystal knew there were worse situations, so she thanked God on a regular. After she decided to suck it up, she buzzed for her doctor. Five minutes later, Dr. O' Conner walked in with a folder in one of his hands.

"Hey, Ms. Simmons, how are you feeling today?" he inquired with a smile.

"I'm blessed, doctor, but I would be even better if I could go home today," Crystal responded sadly.

"Well, today is your lucky day because these are your release papers. You've made a full recovery. You are free to go after signing them."

"Okay. Thank you so much, Dr. O'Conner. I want to apologize because I know that I wasn't your best patient."

"Oh, Ms. Simmons, don't worry. You did well, given your situation. Don't worry about me."

Dr. O'Conner handed her all of the papers to sign, then he helped her sit up in bed. At this point, he realized how beautiful she was. He hadn't really looked at her before then. When she realized he was staring, she smiled, too. Thinking nothing of it, they both continued what they were doing. Shortly after, Crystal was ready to go.

She waited until Dr. O'Conner left the room. Then, she called Destiny. She was so excited when Destiny answered, she felt as if her heart had skipped a beat. Crystal explained everything that happened after she'd left Destiny's house that night. Destiny knew some of it but was not aware of all the details. When Crystal was done, there was silence on the other end. Crystal checked to see if the call had disconnected.

After seeing that it was still connected, she continued. Afterwards, Crystal asked Destiny if she could pick her up in the next hour. Then Crystal finished preparing to leave.

She was surprised to see Destiny waiting for her

in the parking lot with a bear and roses in her hands. Destiny smiled and gave Crystal a hug. She then opened the door to help her into the car.

The ride to Crystal's house was quiet for the most part. She didn't want to ruin the moment; bringing up what had happened would definitely have done just that. Instead, she enjoyed the freedom she now had after being released from the hospital.

When Destiny pulled up to Crystal's apartment, it looked so different to her, but she knew exactly where she was, and she couldn't be happier. The shocking part was, when she entered her place, she thought she had entered someone else's home because everything was clean. There was no longer a mess, which was how she had left it, and the smell of delicious food wafted from her kitchen. As she turned around in her wheelchair to face Destiny, she couldn't help but smile. Destiny returned the smile when she realized that Crystal was trying to figure out how she had gotten into her apartment. Crystal had forgotten about the key she had given her a while back.

Next, Destiny took Crystal to the bathroom where she had a hot bubble bath waiting for her. With the lights off, soft music playing, and candles lit, Crystal, as she bathed, knew that things between them were going to get better. She enjoyed her bath while Destiny prepared her meal. Destiny had prepared baked chicken breast smothered in cream of mushroom soup with yellow rice and green beans for Crystal. Everything was perfect to her, and she hoped Crystal would enjoy it.

When she had finished bathing, Crystal called for Destiny. She was ready for her meal. She waited to get out of the bath tub. When Destiny walked in, Crystal wanted her to make love to her, but she knew she would have to wait for all of that. She had missed her so much, yearned for her touch, her kiss. Just being in her presence

DESTINY IS ALL I NEED

made her heart smile. She had always loved that feeling. Many questions ran through her head while Destiny was there, but she let them float around in her head for the time being. Nothing was coming between her and this feeling. She couldn't get enough. Whatever was wrong, they would soon make it right.

Chapter 9

One Is Good, But Two Is...

Destiny

Destiny had mixed feelings as she spent her day with Crystal. She felt so bad about not going to check on her in the hospital, so she wanted to make it up, but not before she made sure Ashley was straight.

After she got caught the first time, she knew stepping her game up was a must. She thought letting Crystal go would be easy, but, since receiving the call from Dr. O' Conner, her mind had been filled with thoughts of her. Even when Ashley made love to her, Destiny would pretend she was Crystal. At night, while holding Ashley, she couldn't fight the feelings of wanting Crystal.

After realizing how her life had turned into a soap

opera, Destiny continued playing the game two ways. She was not sure how to get out of this mess or if she wanted to. For now, she felt content where she was, and that was in Crystal's arms. She didn't want to leave, especially since she and Ashley weren't on the best of terms because of Crystal, and that had made it easy for her to stay away for days at a time. It appeared that all of the hard work they'd been doing was pointless now.

Destiny knew it was her fault, but what was the point of making an effort if it went unnoticed? She gave herself that much credit. Besides, she knew she wasn't perfect, but she did have needs, too. Maybe, one day, it would work itself out, but, until then, Crystal would do.

These thoughts were on her mind as she enjoyed her last night with Crystal. In the morning, she would be Ashley's fiance again, at least, until another argument came along. Their last night was the best, they went out to eat, had a few drinks, and made love until the morning.

DESTINY IS ALL I NEED

They even made a stop at Starship to make sure their night would be something to remember. Since Crystal was new to this, it was Destiny's pleasure to show her the best toys. They both enjoyed experimenting with the different toys because it made their lovemaking more exciting.

By the end of the night, all of the toys had been put to good use. Destiny knew she had taught Crystal some new shit, and, for her, that was a good thing.

The following morning, Destiny got up at six and took a shower. After she got dressed, she prepared to return home. She knew Ashley would be leaving for work by that time. For Destiny, this was all good. She didn't want to argue that early in the morning.

Chapter 10

The Bigger Woman

Ashley

Ashley wasn't having a good day at work. Her body and mind just weren't up for it, so as she walked out the door, she decided to make the best of it. Usually she loved going to work, but lately, all the sleepless nights had her down. She couldn't concentrate and her work had started to fall behind. Everybody at her workplace had noticed it but didn't ask questions. They respected her and just gave her space.

That day, she had arrived twenty minutes late. And, for the rest of the day, Ashley had drug along. She could only hope that the day went by as quickly as it had come. She hated when she was in this type of mood because usually she was so happy.

The first stop was the break room for a cup of coffee. After that, she went to her office and closed the door.

"Now it's time to get some work done," Ashley stated out loud.

While going through the papers on her desk, Ashley found a note addressed to her that read:

Hello Ashley,

I know you think you have won this battle, but it is far from over. You see, I knew that I wanted Destiny from the first night I saw her, and we are going to be together. You have no idea how Destiny really feels about me. She won't tell you that part. This is not over. We will see each other again!

Crystal

After reading the note, Ashley became confused because she thought Destiny had cut all her ties with Crystal. As the day progressed, those words played over

DESTINY IS ALL I NEED

and over in the back of her mind. She dialed Destiny's number but she never picked up. On the final ring, Ashley waited until the voice-mail came on. She left a very nasty message:

"You and your bitch can have each other! I don't have time to entertain this bullshit, I gave our relationship another chance, but obviously, you are not ready for it."

Ashley hung the phone up. She knew that she and Destiny had been going through it, but she had not thought it was that bad. She did everything in her power not to shed a tear as she put a note on her door and left for the rest of the day. She had refused to let those tears fall because she was and always would be the BIGGER WOMAN!!!

Ashley rushed through the traffic and arrived home in fifteen minutes. There was still no car in the driveway or lights on in the apartment, so she knew

Destiny wasn't there. It was not like she had expected her to be. Hell! Destiny never came home anymore. Now, she understood exactly what was going on— the love of her life was still cheating on her. This was not a good feeling, especially when she had done nothing wrong.

Ashley knew she didn't deserve this and didn't understand why Destiny had proposed to her. Once again, she sat, waiting for Destiny to return. The only difference was, this time, she wasn't going anywhere. She had packed up Destiny's clothes and set them by the front door. There was nothing to talk about.

She took off her engagement ring and sat it on top of everything. This was the first time she had ever taken it off, but she refused to be hurt again. Ashley clearly remembered the way Destiny had behaved at the awards ceremony. Her body was there, but her mind was in another place. They used to have so much fun together— dinners, movies, the whole nine. Lately, the only thing

DESTINY IS ALL I NEED

they did was avoid each other. Sometimes, they made love. Ashley wanted answers but didn't want to argue anymore. She didn't have the energy or the time. If it was over, then let it be. She had given her all, now there was nothing else to give.

Chapter 11

The Check-Up

Crystal

"Who is your doctor, ma'am?" the dark skinned receptionist asked.

"Dr. O'Conner," Crystal answered.

"May I tell him who's here?"

"I'm Ms. Simmons. I have an appointment."

As the receptionist paged Dr. O'Conner, she realized she had seen this woman a few times before. The receptionist wondered how many appointments one patient could have in such a short period of time.

Crystal didn't wait for Dr. O'Conner to respond to the page. She walked straight to Dr. O'Conner's office. You would have thought it was her office the way she sauntered in without a care in the world. Happy to see that he was alone, she gave him a hug and rubbed her hand up and down his back. He returned the favor with no hesitation. The hug lingered on for a few minutes followed by a passionate kiss. They had been secretly dating since Crystal was released from the hospital. Destiny had been taking very good care of her and so had Dr. O' Conner. To her, everybody had a purpose in her life, and she was more than happy with the attention.

Crystal had never had sex with her doctor but right now, she wanted him to take her right there in his office. She made sure he knew that by slowly taking off her shirt, pants, and all of her underclothes. As they dropped to the floor, Crystal saw the look of shock on his face, but she was ready. Dr. O' Conner locked his office door and followed her lead. After removing everything from his desk, Crystal got on top of it, laid back, and waited.

Taking control, Dr. O'Conner kissed her from head to toe, caressing her body. As she anticipated his next move, quiet moans escaped her lips. He teased her body. Her heartbeat increased. As she wondered if he knew she had never been with a man before, she started to panic.

After turning Crystal over on her stomach, Dr. O' Conner was now ready to please her. While rubbing his fingers around her clit, he was surprised at how her body responded to him. She swelled under his touch.

He continued until he heard the wetness of her pussy. He slowly inserted one finger, then two. As he made circular motions in and out, he noticed she was tight, real tight actually.

"Am I your first, Crystal?" he asked.

"Uh…yes, is it a problem?" Crystal questioned.

Instead of answering, he increased the speed of the circular motions he was making with his fingers and grew more aroused as he heard how wet she was getting from his touch. This excited him more than anything, and he knew she was pleased by the way she moaned louder and squirmed around on the desk. After removing his fingers, he slowly inserted himself into her wet pussy. Crystal closed her eyes and whispered, "Go slow, baby."

Then she began to rotate her hips a little. This was a strange feeling at first, but she liked it. She wanted him and liked the way he took his time with her. As they got more into it, she scratched his back as he rubbed his fingers through her hair. Neither wanted to stop, but they knew this wasn't the time or place to really get down. Crystal wanted him to get back to work but not before his tongue showed her pussy some attention.

With two orgasms down, slightly exhausted, Dr. O' Conner gave her what her body was asking for. Now this, she was used to. As his tongue swirled around and around, she threw it back at him. With her legs wrapped around his neck, she was loving this! After orgasm number three, they brought the session to an end.

Dr. O' Conner gathered their clothes and invited

Crystal to his personal shower. Entering together, they couldn't keep their hands off each other. Half of his day was gone already, but he didn't mind at all.

Chapter 12

Choosing Sides

Destiny

Destiny pulled up to her and Ashley's apartment once again at 6:00 A.M. She wasn't expecting to see Ashley, so she took her time going in. To Destiny's surprise, there was Ashley, sitting on the couch, staring blankly at the TV. Destiny wasn't surprised to see her shit packed by the door. Lately, she had been showing Ashley that she didn't want her anymore by staying out days at a time, ignoring her, and running the streets.

When Ashley didn't acknowledge her, she stood in front of the TV.

"Are you high or something? Move!" Ashley snapped.

"We need to talk. Can we talk please?" Destiny

responded.

"Talk about what, Destiny? How you got your bitches leaving notes at my job, or how you stay out all week, like I don't fucking exist? You want to play games, and I'm too old for that, so what the fuck do we have to talk about?"

Destiny just stood there. She could not believe this was Ashley— at least, not the one she used to know. Everything Destiny had done didn't register until now.

As she looked at the pain in Ashley's eyes, she knew this was it for them.

"Ashley, please let me explain!"

"Hell, no! Your shit is at the door! I listened to the lies the first time. I don't want to hear them again. If you want to throw away what we had together, then be my guest."

Destiny pleaded, "But, baby—"

"Baby? Now, Crystal is your baby, not me. She's

DESTINY IS ALL I NEED

probably waiting for you to come back, so you better hurry."

Destiny had lost this battle, so she began to move her belongings to her car. This was not the way she had wanted everything to turn out. She thought she would be doing most of the talking, but Ashley had done that instead. It kind of made her feel better in a way. Besides, ending their relationship wasn't going to be easy. She loved Ashley, but she didn't want to cause her any more pain. The whole thing she had going on with Crystal was confusing her. She didn't know which way to go, yet, Ashley had made it clear which way not to come.

As she loaded her things into her car, she hoped Ashley would come out and talk to her, but she never came out of the house, so Destiny slowly drove to Crystal's house, no longer sure of the decisions she was making.

Chapter 13

Fed-Up

Ashley

Sitting on her couch with her feet propped up on her coffee table, Ashley enjoyed her cup of Hen & Coke. She had thought her days would be spent crying after Destiny left but, to her surprise, she was doing just fine. She had never put on like she wasn't hurt, but she easily could have been much worse since the last six years of her life had been spent with Destiny. Some days were better than others but, overall, she was okay.

Nights were the hardest part since she had grown used to being held while she slept. Every time she pictured Destiny's arms around someone else, she would quickly pull it together. She wasn't sure if she would take Destiny back, if she asked, but, for now, she had a life to live.

Ashley laid back on the sofa and let the Hennessy take over her body. Lifting up a little, she slid down her sexy boy shorts and decided to give herself some pleasure.

Retrieving one of her favorite toys, Ashley gave herself one orgasm after another. As memories of Destiny crept into her mind and heart, tears fell down her cheeks.   She realized right then that, no matter what she said out of her mouth, the heart never lied. The things it felt were the truth; she couldn't deny that. Hating herself for being so weak, Ashley brought her session to an end and fell fast asleep. She hadn't slept in her bed since Destiny left. Instead, she made the living room her comfort zone. Tomorrow would be a new day, bringing new thoughts and feelings. If she was lucky, by then, she'd feel better when it came.

Chapter 14

HAHAHA…..Stupid Bitch

Crystal

Laughing to herself, Crystal relived the day she went for her checkup. Oh, what a pleasant one it was. She couldn't stop thinking about it. After quickly composing herself, thoughts of Destiny surfaced. Their relationship was getting a lot better, but how would she feel about Crystal's other affair?

Crystal didn't think it should be a problem since she'd been the other woman for so long. She was determined to make her presence known, by any means necessary. She dismissed all of that as she jumped into the shower and got ready for Dr. O' Conner. He was taking her to Las Vegas for a week. Since she'd never had this chance before, Crystal was more than ready to

DESTINY IS ALL I NEED

go. This would most definitely be the best time of her life. Crystal turned the water off in the shower.

As she wrapped a towel around her body, she heard talking in her bedroom. Taking quick strides in that direction, she stopped abruptly at the sight of Destiny sitting on her bed. She appeared to be crying, but it was hard to tell. Crystal walked closer and, as she had thought, Destiny was crying. She wrapped her arms around her. Destiny didn't have to explain because Crystal already knew what it was about. Besides, part of it was her fault, but wasn't this what she had always wanted— for Destiny to be hers? So, why was she not taking advantage of the situation?

Destiny cried like a baby in Crystal's arms, until she felt there were no more tears to cry. This was all a fucked up mess. Crystal felt bad because she hadn't wanted Destiny's relationship to end like this. Destiny coming to her like this was too much to handle and now,

DESTINY IS ALL I NEED

what about her trip? Crystal couldn't leave Destiny like this. She had to postpone it until a later date.

After getting Destiny to lie down, she stepped out of the room for a minute. Crystal called Dr. O'Conner and fabricated a story about being sick. He was disappointed but said that he understood. After ending the call, she returned to her bedroom to comfort Destiny. She hated that everything had turned out like this, so she decided to hold the secrets she had for a later day.

After a few minutes, Destiny was sound asleep. Crystal put covers on her and silently walked out of the room. With Destiny there, she had to dismiss any thoughts of Las Vegas. *Damn*, she thought, *DAMN! DAMN! DAMN!*

As she watched a movie in her living room, Crystal began to regret ever pursuing Destiny in the first place. She turned off the movie and walked to her front door. She opened the door and looked at Destiny's car.

DESTINY IS ALL I NEED

When Crystal saw that is was filled with boxes, reality set in. Crystal knew she had to choose. She closed the door and paced the living room floor. Finally, she came up with a plan.

Chapter 15

Crystal Doesn't Love Me

Destiny

The last few weeks at Crystal's house had been pure hell for Destiny. All the attention she had received at the beginning of their relationship had gone out the window. Most of the time, Crystal wasn't even at home, so Destiny was lonely. In addition, she missed Ashley desperately. What a fool she had been.

Now, she couldn't even get a "Hello" on the phone. Ashley had changed her number, so Destiny really felt fucked. Destiny may have done a stupid thing, but she wasn't stupid at all. She had a feeling there was something going on with Crystal. Whenever Crystal saw Destiny approaching and she was on the phone, she would quickly hang up. What was she hiding? Man, life

DESTINY IS ALL I NEED

was going downhill for Destiny it seemed. She had never imagined this happening to her. At one point in her life, Destiny had it made, but now, everything was spiraling out of control, and she didn't know how to stop it. One thing she knew for sure; getting her own place was a must.

Destiny got up and dressed, determined to find an apartment. Time alone was what she really wanted. She had to get her mind right ... ASAP!!!

After riding for hours, Destiny finally called it a day. She had put in four apartment applications. Hopefully, one would be calling her soon. It was time to move on from Crystal because Destiny did not want to be anywhere she wasn't wanted. Destiny was focusing on what she needed to be doing. It was hard enough trying to get used to another woman, let alone, staying with one.

Back at Crystal's house, Destiny noticed that

Crystal wasn't and hadn't been there. No phone calls or anything; Destiny no longer had that pleasure. It didn't feel good when nobody wanted to be bothered with you. It was a hard pill to swallow since she had been the "one" before. As she walked into Crystal's kitchen, Destiny was set on easing her mind for the remainder of the day.

After finding a bottle of vodka, she took shot after shot until she passed out. She woke up hours later when she heard the sound of keys outside the door. Crystal walked in, but she was not alone. There was a man with her.

"What the hell is going on?" Destiny asked as she got off the floor.

After seeing the nonchalant look on Crystal's face, Destiny charged at her and knocked her to the floor. The male behind Crystal stood there, dumbfounded. He didn't know what was happening. After he got over the shock, he tried to help Crystal but was attacked by Destiny's angry blows. Neither of them had a chance with Destiny under all of this stress. The three of them fought like animals, breaking just about everything in the apartment.

When the male, now known as Dr. O'Conner to Destiny, had had just about enough of this madness, he took his phone out and dialed 911, while Crystal and Destiny continued to go at it. The police arrived in time to witness Destiny kicking Crystal in her face. They had to handcuff Destiny in order to question her.

Afterwards, they hauled her off to jail. All she could think about was where she had heard that name before. When it came to her, she was too pissed. She yelled, "YOU DIRTY BITCH!!!" as the police drove off.

In her mind, Crystal would pay for her going to jail and for playing her like a damn fool. All these changes had been because of her, thinking they were going to be together in the end. She had learned the grass wasn't always greener on the other side. Destiny felt stupid. She could have been with the woman that really loved her all of this time. Yet, while trying to straddle the fence, she had caused more issues than she was ready for.

As the police car sped down the highway, her mind drifted off again, over the past six years of her life. It all seemed like a waste of time now that it had ended like this. There was nobody in her corner. Now she had to figure something out.

Chapter 16

Time for Me

Ashley

While sitting in the nail shop, Ashley laid her head back, loving the treatment. As the massage chair tended to her upper and lower back, the masseuse worked miracles on her feet. In her mind's eye, she could see the wonderful days she'd had with Destiny. Everything had been so good before but now, they didn't even talk to each other. Since the day she had put Destiny out, Ashley had been focusing on her own needs. It hadn't been easy, but she had been getting by.

To prevent any more drama from coming into her life, she had changed her number shortly after Destiny left. Ashley was never the one to complain, so she maintained day after day without too much pain. The more days went by, the better she felt.

Unexpectedly, her thoughts were disturbed by the sound of a sexy female's voice asking,

"May I join you?"

Ashley quickly opened her eyes and focused on the woman in front of her. She stared blankly at the woman. She didn't know what to say; her beauty left her speechless.

After finally saying "Yes," Ashley moved her belongings out of the chair next to her. She and the woman made small talk as they received their pampering.

Her name was Carmen. She was slightly taller than Ashley. She had brown skin and dark brown eyes. Her hair was up in a bun, but Ashley could tell that it was long.

As if Carmen was reading her thoughts, she slowly let her hair down. It fell down her back. Ashley thought she was dreaming, just watching this woman. It had been awhile since Destiny had left, so Ashley wanted to feel the touch of a woman again. At the same time, she didn't want to rush into something that she would regret later. As she brought her mind back to the present, Ashley looked at Carmen again, as if she was waiting for her to say something.

"What's the matter? I'm sorry. How rude of me. What's your name?"

"I'm Ashley. It's nice to meet you. It's okay, Carmen. I was enjoying the conversation that we were having, but I wasn't going to let you leave without knowing my name," Ashley replied, flirting with Carmen and not giving a damn who knew it. Carmen followed her lead, and they sat there, talking and flirting for hours.

By the time they were done, it was dark outside, and the nail shop was about to close. Carmen walked Ashley to her car. She opened the door for her and strapped on her seat belt. Ashley couldn't help the smile that crept across her lips. In return, Carmen gave her a sexy smile and a kiss on her hand. Ashley knew she wanted to see Carmen again. She asked for her number before they departed. It took Ashley about thirty minutes to get home, and can you guess what she did when she got there?

BBBBBRRRRIIINNNNNGGG....

BBBBBBRRRRIIINNNNGGGG ....

The phone rang in her ear.

"Hello," Carmen answered.

"Hey, Carmen! It's Ashley. Have you made it home yet?"

"Yes, I just walked through the door. What's up with you?"

"Nothing. I just wanted to make sure you made it home safely," Ashley stated.

This was the beginning of their friendship. Every day, they called or texted each other. They even spent a few lunch breaks together. Ashley felt so good about being able to spend time with Carmen because there was no stress, like she had with Destiny. Nothing was beyond Carmen. She would invite Ashley over to her place, cook her dinner, give her a massage, or they would just chill while watching movies or listening to soft music. Ashley didn't have to do anything while with Carmen.

On one particular night, Carmen invited her to a poetry reading. She asked that Ashley bring everything she needed to prepare except an outfit. At first, Ashley thought this was a joke until Carmen gave her further details. Everything Ashley needed had been bought for her earlier that day. Carmen had purchased matching outfits and shoes for them. After getting dressed, Ashley felt sexier than she had in a long time. Carmen made sure she knew just how sexy she thought she was, too.

The poetry reading started at 8:00 P.M. They arrived at 7:30 P.M. to ensure they would be seated where they wanted to be—in the front. The whole setting was romantic. The lights were down low as soft music played before each poet came to the stage. With each word, it felt like they were being sucked into the poet's world. Sipping Moscato and loving the energy of this scene, Ashley and Carmen felt relaxed and at ease.

For the next two hours, they embraced each other, allowing their minds and bodies to lead them. Although nothing had been confirmed, they both could feel the heat that was steadily moving between them. You would think they'd known each other for years, when it had only been a week. The vibe that the two of them shared was strong and anybody with sense could see that they liked each other.

Between the two, they came to find out that they had so much in common. Once they found these new bonds, they began doing some of those things together. The more time they spent, the more the attraction grew. By the third week, Ashley was ready to take things up a notch. She felt a little weird because she was surprised at how much she was feeling Carmen. Feminine women had never appealed to her, but she was willing to try some new shit.

Most importantly, Carmen made her laugh. That was something she really hadn't done since Destiny. From that day forward, Destiny was history. She would no longer compare anything or anybody TO DESTINY!! That part of her life was over, and she never looked back. She and Carmen were having too much fun together.

By the time they made it back to Ashley's house, it was well after midnight. Ashley didn't want to be alone, so she asked Carmen to spend the night. There was no hesitation with her saying "yes". Although it had been a short period of time, Ashley was ready to move on completely. That night, she and Carmen made love for the first time. It was so good that they both shed tears behind it. At that moment, no words were needed. They were now a couple, and things would be changing for the both of them. It felt good to lay in each other's arms through the night. Neither of them wanted it to end.

Ashley knew she had to return to work the next morning, but she stayed up with Carmen until 4:00 A.M. She felt so brand new and when she arrived at work, everyone around her could tell something had changed. She was so happy and giddy. She was back to the old Ashley they all loved to be around. Carmen promised when Ashley got off work that she would be there, and she was.

When Ashley got home from work, she found that Carmen had cooked dinner and cleaned the whole house. She wanted to make sure there was nothing Ashley had to do other than chill. It was amazing how Ashley's life had changed. She had just been feeling sorry for herself over all the craziness that had gone on between her and Destiny. Now, look at her. Her life had really changed. That was worth smiling about.

Chapter 17

Vegas, Here We Come

Crystal

The day after all that shit with Destiny went down, Crystal was still ready for her trip to Las Vegas. Her man had planned it perfectly, and she wasn't going to let him down again. All she needed to take on the trip was herself. Everything else would be bought en route to their destination.

David O'Conner had turned out to be the man of her dreams. The best thing about being with him was that he was all hers. There was no sharing. He took care of Crystal to the fullest. He had arranged for her to move in with him when they returned from Las Vegas. That gave them even more to look forward to. There was no way in hell David was going to let Crystal go. Anybody who tried to get in the way would have to pay the price.

He was a little early picking her up. He told her they had to make love before the trip. At first, Crystal was worried about them being late until he assured her they wouldn't be.

Following his instructions, Crystal laid spread eagle on her soft bed as she anticipated his arrival. David walked into the apartment with a small bottle of chocolate syrup and strawberries in hand. She would be his dessert before dinner that evening.

Stopping to heat the chocolate in a bowl, David quickly made his way to the bedroom. They wasted no time getting it on until they both were winded. The way they screamed and called out each other's names, you would've thought no one existed in the world but them. David was hitting all the right spots that Crystal loved; when she felt as if she couldn't take anymore, he would put that ass in another position. Since she was never one to turn down a challenge, Crystal obliged, making David want more and more.

Now that they felt secure with each other, they no long used condoms. Neither of them were ready for parenthood, so they promised to be careful until they were. They went at each other like it was their first time. They weren't ready to stop but knew they had to. Crystal felt like a brand new woman when she was with David. She never knew that love could feel this good.

Whether they were making love or having a night out on the town, she cherished every moment. Times like this made her think back to the day David had introduced her to his family. Everyone was excited to see who had captured his heart. He had never brought a woman home before, so they knew Crystal had to be special.

After sharing the story about how they had met, his family really fell in love with her, especially his mother Mrs. O'Conner. Although she asked a thousand questions, she still welcomed Crystal into their family. Mrs. O'Conner's biggest concern was their age difference; David was ten years her senior.

For the past few months, they had only grown closer, which was a good sign in his mother's eyes. As she let those memories drift away, Crystal looked over at David, sleeping beside her. She kissed his lips, teasing him.

"Damn, baby, did I work that ass or what?" she boasted.

"Don't be funny. You know I'm OVERWORKED!!! You have too much energy for me," David replied, trying to get his body to obey his commands.

"You asked for it, coming in here with your chocolate and strawberries. You know that shit turned me on, baby, especially when you put that strawberry in your mouth, devouring it while you mixed its juices with mine, umm, umm, umm!!!"

"Alright, alright, baby, are we taking this trip or what? Because, if you keep talking like that, we are going to miss out," David teased her as he smacked her on the ass.

David and Crystal continued to flirt as they prepared to leave, which didn't take long since they weren't taking anything from home. Shortly after, they were both ready. They headed out the door.

Chapter 18

Sitting In a Cold Cell

Destiny

Day Number Seven

Destiny was still sitting in a cold cell. Her release was dependent upon Crystal, but nobody could contact her.

Where the hell is she? Frustrated wasn't the word to describe the way Destiny felt and the fact she had no one in her corner didn't make it better.

She understood that things had gotten out of hand at Crystal's, but how could she play her like that? Everything around Destiny was falling apart. She needed to get out of jail to clear her thoughts. This was no place for her— the hard beds, cold meals, and people always telling her what to do. Destiny played by nobody's rules but her own. Right now, she wished that she could contact Ashley, just to see how she was doing and to hear her voice. Hoping she would receive a letter within a couple of days, Destiny wrote:

Dear Ashley,

How are you? I'm sure you don't want to talk to me, but I just wanted to see how you were doing. We shared the best six years of my life together. I know I fucked up. That's the reason I won't ask you to take me back, but I, at least, want to be friends. When you received this letter, I am sure you were able to tell that I'd gotten into some trouble by the address.

Please Ashley, contact me. I need a friend right now. I'm not trying to interfere in your life or interrupt it. If you can find it in your heart to forgive me, I promise you I won't fuck up our friendship the way I did our relationship.

I hope that this letter finds you in a better

position than what I'm in right now.

Love Always,

Destiny

While folding the letter, Destiny thought about not sending it, but she needed someone to talk to. Hopefully, Ashley would contact her after she received the letter.

She felt like the weight of the world was holding her body hostage, she laid down and tried to figure out a way to escape the madness she called her life.

As the past few months played back in her head, Destiny shed more tears. It seemed like the only sensible thing to do. If this was life, she didn't feel like she wanted any part of it.

When it was lunchtime, Destiny thought it was time to talk to some of the other inmates to see if they could hook her up with some pills. Her life was hell right now; all she wanted to do was ease the pain she felt.

DESTINY IS ALL I NEED

Destiny walked in line to the jail's cafeteria.

When she arrived, she saw a group of thuggish looking dudes standing together. She walked up to them and boldly asked if they knew where she could get some ecstasy. One dude, who everybody called Lil Red. looked at her funny at first then told her to follow him. They went off into another corner where he handed her a small plastic bag filled with tiny red pills.

In return, Destiny handed him some balled up bills that she had been able to stash at the time of her arrest. This would be something new for her but she was ready to explore.

After lunch, she rushed back to her cell. She stared at the pills for a long time and decided to wait until lights out to pop them. She had forgotten about the letter to Ashley. It had fallen down the side of her bed.

****

The next morning, when they called for the inmates

to come for breakfast, Destiny didn't make it. When they went to get her, one of them discovered that she was unresponsive. The ambulance was called to make sure she was okay. She spent the rest of the night in the hospital and was put under surveillance because the doctors discovered that she had taken four EX pills at once. It was a sad situation, being that she was so young.

One thing was for certain, though she was going through some shit that needed to be handled, having to go back to jail wasn't something she looked forward to, but she understood that there was no other choice.

Before leaving the hospital, Destiny called Crystal again. This time, she answered and promised to be down to the jail within two hours to have the charges dropped. Neither of them indulged in a conversation about "them" because it was obvious that their relationship was over, too.

Crystal was okay with that since she had David to be

everything Destiny hadn't been, but Destiny was not mentally ready for any kind of relationship. The only good thing she had going on was being released from that cold cell.

Chapter 19

Life after Destiny

Ashley

Ashley's life was now going in a brighter direction. All of the things she dreamed of doing were now happening and Carmen was the person to thank for that. They did everything together.

On one particular day, it was raining, so Carmen and Ashley decided to chill and watch a couple of movies. They went to the corner store to pick up something to drink. As they got out of the car, they saw a dusty looking woman. She walked up to their car, calling Ashley's name. She and Carmen looked at each other, then at the lady.

"Ashley! Ashley! Come here! It's Destiny!"

"Destiny? It can't be. What the fuck happened to

you?" Ashley said, still confused.

As Ashley walked closer, she could see that Destiny was strung out on something. Her lips were chapped and had white crust at the corners; her mane was unkempt, making her appear older than she really was. The clothes she had on were dirty, as well as her shoes. Destiny also smelled horribly. You could tell that she had been drinking non-stop. The stench of sweat and alcohol oozed from her pores. The only thing Ashley could do was shake her head but when she turned to walk away, a single tear fell from her eye.

Her heart plunged at the sight of Destiny because she had been in love with her for six years. At the same time, Ashley felt that there was nothing she could do. Destiny looked as if she was already too far gone. Leaving her outside that store made Ashley feel bad, but she wasn't in the mood for that shit.

Carmen asked questions on the way back home,

DESTINY IS ALL I NEED

and Ashley told her they would talk when they got there. As they pulled out of the parking lot, she heard Destiny asking people for spare change. Carmen turned the car around, called Destiny to the car, and gave her a twenty dollar bill. Ashley was confused, wondering why she had done that, knowing drugs would be bought with the money. Instead of asking, Ashley remained quiet while her thoughts drifted off. Talk about killing the mood. The incident had ruined Ashley's night, and, when they got home, she told Carmen everything.

She also told Carmen that she wanted to help Destiny, if it was possible. Carmen didn't have a problem with it; she would do anything for Ashley. Because the mood was gone, the two went to bed early. Around 2:00 A.M., Ashley woke up in a cold sweat, crying and hugging her pillow. When Carmen woke up, she held Ashley in her arms. Ashley shared the bad dream she'd had.

DESTINY IS ALL I NEED

"Baby, it was terrible, and it seemed so real! I'm afraid that something bad has happened to her. She was calling my name in the dream as if she was hurt. When I walked up to her, she was bleeding everywhere. There was so much blood!" Ashley explained.

"Slow down, baby, slow down… who is 'she'?" Carmen asked.

"Destiny. It was Destiny. She's hurt. I know it."

"Calm down. We will try to find her. Hopefully, she's still in the area where we saw her the first time."

Ashley was surprised at how she was reacting. It was obvious that she still cared about Destiny. Although their relationship was over, she still felt the need to help.

Ashley stayed up for another hour and a half. Then, she was finally able to get some sleep. When she woke up later that morning, she still didn't feel right. It was one thing to have a bad dream, but this one was recurring.

DESTINY IS ALL I NEED

She and Carmen got ready to head to the store they had visited the night before. Looking for Destiny was a task; there were so many people standing around that it was hard to see. As soon as Ashley stepped out of the car, she could hear people talking about someone being shot. There was yellow tape around one part of the store; no one was allowed in that area.

As they moved closer, Ashley saw Destiny lying on the ground with blood all around her. The only thing she remembered from that point was falling backwards, into Carmen's arms. Everything else was a blur. Carmen didn't know what to do, and she wasn't in a position to ask any questions. It took about ten minutes for Ashley to realize what was going on. By this time, Carmen had her in the car because everybody had to leave the premises.

Chapter 20

This Isn't Living

Destiny

After seeing Ashley at the store, Destiny felt as if everything was fucked up. The last thing she wanted was for Ashley to see her strung out like that. All she wanted to do was tell Ashley how sorry she was for messing up what they'd had, but when Ashley walked away, that really tore her apart inside. She needed a friend, not twenty fucking dollars. That was the reason she was laid up in the hospital, once again.

It was right before dawn. She'd spent that same twenty on more pills and alcohol. The dude who was supplying her knew she owed him money and wanted it by any means necessary. Destiny explained that she didn't have any more money, but she would get it before the day was over. While hanging around the store, Destiny begged people for money, but they weren't giving her shit. When she finally grew tired of asking, she decided she would take it from whomever she thought she could, but the blade she carried for protection wasn't enough to protect her from a gun. She had tried to steal from the wrong person!

Her plan was to pick pocket hustlers that hung out at the store, but her plan didn't go as planned and one of the boys shot her. They were long gone before the police came. with Destiny being too high to identify anybody.

As she lay in the hospital bed, all she could think about was how dumb she had been. Even if she had gotten away with stealing the wallet, they still would have been looking for her ass and finding her wouldn't have been hard to do. This was it.

Destiny needed help when she was released, so she decided to check into a Rehab facility. Hopefully, after treatment, she could get back on the right track. All the drinking and pill popping had led her to a dead end. It was up to her to find her way out. Feeling like this made her wish she was still with Ashley. Together, they would have made it through anything. Somewhere along the way, Destiny had to pull it together because those days were long gone.

****

Two hours later, Destiny's doctor came in and told her there were two visitors there for her. Since she was not expecting anyone, she wondered who it could possibly be. When Ashley and Carmen walked in, Destiny felt happy and confused at the same time.

As Ashley walked to the bed and grabbed her hand, Carmen stood by the door. Ashley explained that she and Carmen would be helping her once she was released. At first, Destiny was about to go off, feeling like Ashley was only there because she felt sorry for her. Then Destiny quickly changed her mind when she saw Ashley crying. She then realized that Ashley still cared about her. All this time, Destiny didn't think anyone did.

When Ashley was done talking, she and Carmen left as quickly as they had come. Destiny was once again left with her own thoughts and feelings to deal with. The only difference was, this time, she would take someone else's advice. Maybe this was what she needed. Maybe her life could be pulled together after all. Ashley's presence made Destiny feel like all was not lost.

Holding the card Ashley had handed to her, she realized that it was Ashley's business card. It was slightly different from the last time she had seen it. Of course, the contact information was different, but it also included Carmen Jones's information. Right then, Destiny knew that the two of them were living her dream. She had always wanted to be Ashley's partner, but that would never happen now.

DESTINY IS ALL I NEED

As she tried to put those thoughts in the back of her mind, she decided to keep the card anyway. This was what she needed and she would be a fool to let it pass her by.

As tears poured from Destiny's eyes, she knew that, this time, they were not tears of pain and sadness, but tears of joy and a new beginning. These would be the last tears she shed for a while because she was ready to put in the work to get her life back. No more "petty" for Destiny.

DESTINY IS ALL I NEED

Part One Reader's Guide Questions

1.   What are the lessons that you found most important?

2.   Are you like any of the characters in *Destiny Is All I Need*? How?

3.   If you were Destiny, would you have given up on the struggles that she faced?

4.   What character did you like the most? Why?

5.   From the title of the book, did you think "Destiny" was speaking of a person or "Destiny" as in finding your way?

6.   Which character is featured in the Prologue?

Part Two

Chapter 21

Carmen's Plot

Destiny nervously paced the floor of the lobby as she waited for Ashley to pick her up. All she wanted to do was get some fresh air but she had to admit that seeing Ashley again wouldn't be bad either. It had been a few days since her last visit.

Although she wasn't alone, it was a pleasure just to see her face, but that thought diminished when Destiny saw Carmen walk through the door. Disappointment was displayed on her face. Instantly, Destiny dropped her head and swiftly headed to the door, ready to leave.

"Wow! I didn't know you'd be so happy to see me," Carmen sarcastically stated.

"It's just…I thought Ashley would be with you, but I

do appreciate you coming to get me. I'm ready to get out of here."

"That's cool. Well, I can't wait for you to see the apartment we found for you, and you don't have to worry about rent because it's paid up for six months."

"Thank you, but you and Ashley didn't have to do that for me."

"Ashley doesn't know about the rent part, but we did pick out the apartment together, since she knows what you like."

"Why wouldn't you tell her about the rent?"

As they got into Carmen's car, Carmen ignored Destiny's question and instead, told her to just relax because she had everything under control. Next, she drove a short distance to the nearest liquor store and parked the car. Destiny felt herself get anxious as she sat in the passenger seat. This was one place that she didn't need to be because drugs and alcohol were like Siamese twins for her. Destiny wondered what Carmen was up to since she already knew this wasn't the right place for her.

When she looked at Carmen, she saw that a mischievous smile had spread across her face, and, with that same smile plastered on her face, Carmen stepped out of the car and went into the store. As soon as she entered the liquor store, Destiny noticed that she had left her cell phone behind.

Nervously, Destiny picked it up and dialed Ashley's number. Something didn't feel right about this whole situation. She could feel it in the pit of her stomach. The phone rang several times before she heard Ashley's sweet voice, telling her callers to leave a detailed message at the tone.

By the time Carmen came back out, Destiny had placed her cell phone back on the seat. She truly wished Ashley would have picked up the phone because Destiny didn't know what else to do and Carmen was her only means of transportation.

After maneuvering out of the parking spot, Carmen drove them to Destiny's new apartment in Stone Mountain. It was a very small place, but Destiny didn't have any complaints. She had everything that she needed.

The apartment was fully furnished, and everything was perfect. In her small living room, she had a black leather sectional with matching end tables; while the carpet was trimmed in black and gold with a huge tiger in the middle, the walls were decorated with paintings that complimented the rest of the furniture. There was a flat screen TV that accompanied a stereo in an entertainment system.

Destiny walked through the rest of the apartment in awe as she saw how everything was so nicely set up. It was only one bedroom, but that was all she needed. Destiny thought that the bedroom would be her favorite spot. She had a king sized bed that sat in the middle of the floor. This was what she had longed for—to be in her own bed. Carmen closely watched her every move as she followed behind her.

"Do you like your apartment?"

"Yes! This shit is hot!"

"I'm happy to see that you like it. We took some time to set this all up for you. Ashley knew you would be surprised."

"Thank you. I don't know how I will ever repay the two of you for doing this for me."

"Oh, don't worry about that now. We can talk about it later. Everything that you need is right here in this apartment. We even bought you some new clothes and shoes. We know how hard shit has gotten for you, so we wanted to make sure you were straight. We bought everything that you need, all the way down to your socks."

Destiny nodded her head. She was at a loss for words. She continued her journey around her new place as Carmen went into the kitchen to fix them some drinks. It was time to put her plan into motion.

When Destiny made it back into her bedroom, Carmen was laying back on the bed, wearing nothing but a pair of red and black thongs and a black lace bra. Destiny couldn't help but notice how nicely her breasts sat up in the bra, but she knew it wasn't right. *What the hell is going on?* She wondered.

"You should come and have a drink with me. I know you have been under a lot of stress lately," Carmen said as she stared at Destiny.

"No. This isn't cool, Carmen. I'm supposed to be getting my life back on track and…and …well, you know…"

Destiny's words trailed off as she continued to look at Carmen, sitting there, looking good enough to eat,

DESTINY IS ALL I NEED

and the drink Carmen held in her hand didn't help. Destiny could almost taste it just by looking at it. Even though Destiny knew better, that didn't stop her from joining Carmen on the bed.

As Destiny climbed onto the bed and got comfortable, Carmen could hardly contain her excitement. This was just what she had been hoping for. She never let Destiny's glass get empty. She just kept the drinks coming. By the fourth drink, Destiny was feeling way too good. Carmen used this to her advantage and slid closer to Destiny. She whispered softly in her ear, but Destiny couldn't make out any of the words.

Chapter 22

In Between the Sheets

The next morning, Destiny woke with Carmen's head between her legs. She tried to move her legs, but they were held down by Carmen's weight. While looking around the dark room, Destiny tried to figure out what the hell had happened, but an unforgiving migraine prevented her from thinking straight. The only thing she remembered was having some drinks, but it appeared that she had had too many. Finally, she threw the sheets back and tapped Carmen, who moved slightly but didn't wake up.

"Shit!"

Destiny said out loud as she forcefully moved Carmen so that she could get up.

After moving Carmen, Destiny made her way to

the bathroom. She turned the hot water on in the shower.

Last night was a night that I don't remember, but I will probably never forget it, she thought as she stood under the steaming hot water.

She tried to recall the previous night's events, but nothing made any sense to her. She continuously shook her head as the water eased her headache.

After she was done, she turned the water off, wrapped herself in a towel, and went back to her bedroom where she found Carmen sitting on the edge of the bed, looking how Destiny felt.

"Carmen, what the hell happened?" Destiny asked, while grabbing some clothes from the drawer.

"I gave you what you asked for, then we went to sleep."

"I didn't ask for shit! What kind of game are you playing?"

"I'm not playing games with you. I have a plan

DESTINY IS ALL I NEED

that's going to benefit both of us in the end, and you just made it easier by falling into my trap. Now, I see why Ashley was so in love with you but, after she finds out we slept together, she will come back to me and forget all about you."

"No! This can't be right, and what do you mean 'she will come back' to you? The two of you were just together when I was in the hospital."

"She wants you, Destiny, and I want her," Carmen calmly said as she made her way to the bathroom to shower.

As soon as Carmen stepped into the shower, Destiny frantically searched through Carmen's belongings, looking for her cell phone. She found it clipped to the side of her pants. Without wasting any time, she dialed Ashley's number but, again, there was no answer. This time, she took it a step further by calling her work number and luckily, that was where she was

DESTINY IS ALL I NEED

able to reach her.

Destiny kept her voice low as she told Ashley to come to her apartment. She wanted her to catch Carmen there. She wasn't going to get played like a fool because she had a trick of her own. She could see what this was all about. Carmen was trying to set her up, so Ashley would think she was the bad one. That way, the two of them could be together. Carmen just wanted Destiny out of the picture completely.

****

When Carmen came out of the bathroom, she was wrapped in just a towel. She laid across the bed in her birthday suit. Destiny was pissed off and didn't have anything to say to her. She just waited for Ashley, so she could get the hell away from this crazy bitch.

Destiny left Carmen in the bedroom and went to the living room. She cut on the TV. It seemed like forever passed as she waited for Ashley. When she finally heard a soft knock at the door, she eased the front door open and quietly crept out.

Carmen walked to the living room. She already knew Destiny was gone, but she didn't know who she had left with until she picked up her cell phone. This was not a part of her plan.

Even though she knew she wasn't going to answer her calls, Carmen dialed Ashley's number back to back. All she wanted to do was talk to her. Was that too much to ask? She felt like a fool. After all they had been through, Carmen couldn't understand why Ashley wanted to be with Destiny. They had been good until Destiny came with all of her issues. That was when Ashley told Carmen that things were moving too fast for her and she couldn't just leave Destiny at the time she needed her most.

On the day they left the hospital, Ashley could see the pain in Destiny's eyes. When they got back to

DESTINY IS ALL I NEED

Carmen's place, Ashley broke the bad news to her, and Carmen showed a side of herself that Ashley had never seen before. She yelled and threw shit all over the apartment. A few times, Ashley thought Carmen was going to hit her. Instead of causing her more aggravation, Ashley gathered her things and left.

Chapter 23

Destiny & Ashley

While Ashley drove, Destiny told her about what had occurred after Carmen picked her up. There was no easy way to explain that she had slept with Carmen while she was under the influence, but Destiny told it all; the parts she remembered anyway. Ashley didn't seem to be mad, but Destiny could tell something was wrong. Her forehead was etched with worry lines as she stared straight ahead. She would occasionally put her finger against her chin as if she was thinking hard. Destiny knew what that gesture meant because they had spent six years together. Even though it pained her, Ashley took in all of the details that Destiny told her.

When they pulled up at the house they once shared, they finally looked at each other. It had been awhile since

DESTINY IS ALL I NEED

Destiny had been there, and she didn't feel right. Ashley placed her hand on top of Destiny's to let her know it was okay.

As they walked to the front door, Ashley talked about what had happened between her and Carmen. By the time they were inside, Destiny was already tired of hearing about her. Carmen's words floated around in her head:

"I have a plan that's going to benefit the both of us at the end. You just made it easier by falling into my trap."

****

Damn! If I had never done all that shit, Ashley would have never come in contact with Carmen. This is my fault, Destiny thought to herself as she watched Ashley go towards the kitchen.

Her heart sank as she watched Ashley pull a little white bag out of her purse. She could see the white substance from where she stood. Destiny knew it was cocaine. Ashley took her pinky nail and put it inside the bag. She put the cocaine up to her nose and took a long sniff. She had a chance to do this one more time before Destiny made her way over to her and snatched the bag from her hand. Because the drug had already taken effect on her, Ashley didn't have time to respond.

"What the fuck are you doing, Ashley?" Destiny yelled.

"Nothing. I'm just having a little fun. It's been a long day."

"Do you have any more drugs on you? I can't sit back and watch you do this shit!"

"No, but I know where to get them from."

Destiny didn't know what to say. She wasn't sure if this was something she could handle. She hadn't even gotten the help she needed, and, now, Ashley was messing around with drugs, too.

DESTINY IS ALL I NEED

This has to be a habit she picked up from that bitch Carmen! Destiny thought, feeling her anger rise. Ashley walked to her bedroom and closed the door behind her, leaving Destiny to figure out what the hell was going on.

Destiny took a seat on the sofa and just looked at the drugs she had taken from Ashley. There was so much shit going on. Even though she wanted to be the strong one, she took her index finger and dipped it inside the bag and did what she had just yelled at Ashley for doing.

It didn't take long for it to make her body numb. Destiny laid her head back and closed her eyes as sleep consumed her.

****

Destiny woke up hours later to the sound of Ashley's laughter. She knew she had been asleep for a while because it was now dark outside. She got up and went to the bedroom where she found Ashley lying across the bed watching *Martin*. Destiny immediately noticed how her chocolate ass sat firmly in a pair of cream colored boy shorts. Memories flooded her mind as she reminisced about their past. She joined Ashley on the bed and watched the rest of *Martin*, but she felt awkward. Everything felt so different between them. So much had changed. Once the show ended, Destiny told Ashley they needed to talk.

"What do you want to talk about?"

"We need to talk about us and what we plan on doing about this relationship, if there is going to be one."

"Wait! What do you mean 'if'? I have stood by you through everything. You mean to tell me you can't hold me down now that—"

"Hold on! Hold on! You are moving way too fast..."

"I never said anything like that. I'm talking about the drugs and shit, Ashley. I got caught up in a lot of shit

DESTINY IS ALL I NEED

behind them, and I don't want you to go down the same road. Who turned you on to that shit? Was it Carmen?"

"Baby, none of that matters now. You and I need to work on our relationship. I don't want to live in the past."

"It's not that easy, Ashley. We have been through a lot, and, in order for us to move forward, we have to address these issues."

Ashley held her head down for a minute as she tried to figure out where to start. A lot had happened since their break-up, and she wasn't sure if Destiny would understand.

As she sat up on the bed, she decided to just start from the beginning and tell everything. She explained how her relationship with Carmen had played out, the reason they weren't together anymore, and how the drugs had come into play. Destiny felt bad after hearing that she was part of the reason Ashley had started fucking around with them. Ashley had been under a lot of stress when Destiny was in the hospital, and Carmen had kept pressuring her to move forward with their relationship. Then Carmen introduced her to "powder", telling her that it would make her feel better. They would get high together and sex each other down, but Ashley's heart was still with Destiny.

Despite all they had been through, Ashley couldn't go any further with Carmen. Ashley went on to explain how hard it was to shake Carmen, but she still wanted Destiny, no matter what.

Destiny sat there and listened quietly, but she grew angrier by the minute. She had to admit that all of this was her fault. She never interrupted Ashley as she spoke, instead, she listened. At the same time, she thought of ways to make shit better between them. It wasn't until she saw tears forming in Ashley's eyes that she stopped her, grabbed and held her close.

DESTINY IS ALL I NEED

Destiny apologized over and over again. She felt the pain surfacing from every mistake she had made. Now that Ashley was willing to give their relationship another chance, she couldn't fuck up again. They held each other until they both drifted off to sleep.

Shortly before dawn, they both were awakened by the ringing of Ashley's cell phone. It was Carmen. Destiny reached over and sent the call to voice-mail. Then they went back to sleep. They woke up again around nine.

After doing the morning ritual, Ashley prepared breakfast for them because she knew Destiny loved her cooking. *What better way to get us back on track?* Ashley thought.

After making sausages, cheese eggs and biscuits, they sat down to eat. Ashley's phone rang non-stop the entire time and it pissed Destiny off.

Carmen just won't stop, Destiny thought, so she

DESTINY IS ALL I NEED

answered the phone the next time it rang. The conversation quickly got heated. Carmen was mad that her plan hadn't worked. They yelled and cursed at each other until Ashley couldn't take it anymore. She gestured for Destiny to hang up the phone. There was no need to argue with Carmen's simple ass. It was over between them and that was all that mattered. Ashley just wanted to move on.

Chapter 24

Crystal Returns

Ashley and Destiny prepared to go the main Metro PCS store, so they could get Ashley's number changed. They showered together and made love under the hot water before heading out. It had been so long, but the feeling was familiar. Their bodies seemed to be in tune with each other and they could feel their hearts reconnecting. After the episode in the shower, they dried each other off, headed to their bedroom, and got dressed.

Destiny threw on a pair of blue jean shorts and a white tank, while Ashley put on a pair of capris and a tank top with the word DIVA written across the front. Ashley grabbed her purse, and they headed out the door.

As soon as she opened the front door, Ashley found Crystal standing there, looking as if she had lost her best friend. Ashley stood there, looking at her. At the same time, she wondered why the hell she was there in the first place. Ashley wanted to go the fuck off, but the look in Crystal's eyes spoke volumes. She knew Crystal needed some help. Her light colored face was moist from the tears she had cried on the way over to them.

Destiny walked up behind Ashley and said,

"Baby, are you ready to…"

Her words trailed off upon seeing Crystal. Their eyes met for a brief second until Destiny looked away.

"I didn't come here to start anything. I just need somebody to talk to," Crystal stated.

"What's the matter?" Ashley asked.

Destiny had already walked away from the door. She couldn't believe Crystal was there.

"My life has been a total wreck since Destiny and I stopped messing around, and I just needed some closure. I think a lot of things that happened could have

DESTINY IS ALL I NEED

been avoided if we had only handled things differently. I just wanted to tell the both of you that I apologize for the trouble I caused."

Ashley stood there, dumbfounded, not really knowing what to say. She couldn't go off on Crystal, not when she was standing there pouring her heart out. Destiny was now at the door again. Crystal's words had the same effect on her as they'd had on Ashley. The three of them had been through so much but, at the end of the day, everybody needed closure so Ashley invited Crystal into their home.

After Crystal accepted Ashley's invitation, they went inside, sat down and had a long talk. For the most part, Ashley and Destiny listened as Crystal told them about everything that was going on. She told them that the man she thought was going to be her husband had left her after she had confessed about her relationship with Destiny. He said he couldn't let his friends and family know that he was planning to marry an ex-lesbian. He felt that she would no longer make a good wife for him. Besides, he was a successful doctor, and he didn't want his relationship with her to tarnish his reputation. She went on to say that, after they returned from Las Vegas, they went their separate ways and she hadn't heard from him since. That was almost three months ago. All of the plans they had made, when they returned, hadn't happened and Crystal was devastated. She had to go back to her one bedroom apartment, where she had spent most of her time, sulking. It was obvious that David wasn't coming back.

Before Crystal realized it, tears were falling from her eyes again. Ashley walked over to her and wrapped her in a tight embrace. She rubbed her back slowly. Destiny just stood there. She could not believe what she was seeing. Just awhile back, they had been ready to tear each other's limbs apart. She took this time and went to the kitchen to fix them some alcoholic beverages. She knew Ashley well, so finding a bottle of Hennessy sitting next to the microwave wasn't a surprise. She grabbed three glasses from the counter and poured each of them a shot. She filled hers to the rim thinking *I need this shit!*

She made her way back to the living room where she found Ashley and Crystal still sitting on the sofa next to each other. Now there was soft music coming from the speakers. The five disc changer played various songs by some of their favorite artists. Ashley was really into R&B music. The songs switched from **Ginuwine** to **Avant** to **Donnell Jones**. By the time it got to the next artist, they were all in a zone and on their second cups of Hen.

Crystal got up from the sofa and walked over to Ashley. She stood in front of her and slowly undid the buttons on her shirt. She allowed it to fall down to her waist, exposing her perfect A-cup breasts that sat up in a

DESTINY IS ALL I NEED

black lace bra that was trimmed in purple. She did the same with the jeans that she wore. Ashley's eyes followed Crystal's hand movements. She peeped the matching boy shorts that Crystal was wearing. Then, Ashley's eyes traveled back to the succulent strawberry that was tatted on her left breast. Destiny sat there, in a daze, just watching. She could feel her pussy getting wet just from watching the two of them—the woman she was in love with and the one she used to be in love with. This was a dream come true for her, so who was she to stop them?

Ashley reached up and grabbed Crystal by her neck and brought her lips to hers. They kissed like old lovers. Their tongues did a slow dance as they tasted the Hen on each other's breathe. Ashley took control and took a tour all over Crystal's body, up and down her back, and all over her ass. She finally stopped at her breasts.

As she cupped her breasts, the heat rose in the room,

and no one wanted to turn it down. Crystal was still standing in front of Ashley, so she started to undress her as well. As their clothes formed a mountain in the middle of the living room floor, Destiny enjoyed the show with a seductive look in her eyes. When Ashley realized that Destiny was not participating, she pulled away from Crystal for a minute. Ashley sensually walked over to Destiny and took her clothes off, too.

Once everyone was completely naked, they moved their party to the bedroom. Ashley told Destiny to lay down on the bed. She went down and positioned herself between her legs. Crystal straddled Destiny's face while holding the headboard. Thirty minutes in, you couldn't tell them apart, the only sounds in the room were their moans that echoed from wall to wall. The sounds of the moans were intoxicating to each of their ears. Time crept along, but neither one seemed to be concerned. They switched positions frequently to make

DESTINY IS ALL I NEED

sure no one was left out of the pleasure.

Now, Destiny sat up on the bed and watched Ashley and Crystal go at it. Crystal was laying between Ashley's legs with her face buried deep into her pussy. Her clit throbbed as she licked and sucked on Ashley; they were having a ball. Those drinks had really brought out the freak in all them.

In addition to using her tongue, Crystal inserted two fingers into her and slowly moved them in and out. Ashley's juices were all over her fingers. Destiny moved closer to them and sucked Crystal's fingers, devouring the flavor as their moans increased. They took a quick break just to get more drinks. This was going to be a good day after all.

When they were finally finished, the three of them laid in bed, cuddled up under each other. Destiny felt like a BOSS as she laid between the two of them. What more could a woman ask for? It had been one crazy-ass day, but it had all been worth it. Ashley, Destiny, and Crystal had their own thoughts on their brains as they drifted off to sleep.

Chapter 25

Leave Us Alone

Crystal spent the rest of the day shopping at South DeKalb Mall with Ashley and Destiny. Ashley and Crystal enjoyed going in and out of the different stores and dragging Destiny along the whole way. She wasn't into all the girly stores they went in, but they made it up to her. Thanks to all of the stuff that had been left with Carmen was replaced, Ashley made sure she had everything she needed. Crystal even bought her some things to add to her collection.

When they went into the food court to grab a bite to eat, everyone looked at them strangely, wondering what type of relationship they had. The three of them held hands as they walked through the mall and dared anybody to say something. When they left the mall,

DESTINY IS ALL I NEED

Ashley and Crystal dropped Destiny off first. Then the two went to the get their hair and nails done. There was no way they were going to make Destiny suffer through that. Dominant women hated sitting around at the beauty parlor and nail shop. This gave Ashley and Crystal a chance to really get to know each other on another level.

Ashley told Crystal about her job and all of the plans she had. They even talked about going into business together, and of course, Destiny would be a part too.

When they arrived at the beauty salon, it was jam-packed, and they knew they would be there for a while. After a thirty minute wait, Ashley told her beautician how she wanted her hair and Crystal did the same.

Ashley's hair was in a short cut with tight curls in the back and a Mohawk down the middle. That shit was laid to perfection. Crystal had her hair layered in soft curls that fell to the middle of her back. Afterwards, they headed to the nail shop where they talked more. They were so into the conversation, they didn't see Carmen approaching them. Ashley looked up into her angry eyes and did a double take.

Carmen looked like hell frozen over. The attractive woman that she used to know was gone and had been replaced by this monster in front of her. Carmen's clothes and shoes were dirty. Her hair was unkempt, and you could tell she hadn't had a bath recently. Ashley just stared at her. No words were spoken between the two. Crystal looked at the woman standing in front of them and shook her head at the sight of her. She wondered what kind of relationship Ashley had with her.

Ashley's tone was soft but firm as she stated, "Carmen, I want you to leave us alone. There is nothing else between you and me. What we had is over. I don't want you calling, texting, or coming around my house anymore. You are a person that I used to think differently of, but you turned out to be all wrong for me. This is the end of us..."

"You tried to use Destiny, thinking it was going to work in your favor, but you lost. She is my woman and always will be, so you can turn right around and walk out the door the same way you came in."

Carmen stood there, embarrassed and feeling sorry for herself. When she had seen Ashley and Crystal, she thought that was her chance to make things right. She hadn't considered her appearance or anything else. All she wanted to do was have Ashley back in her life. That was the reason she had tried to play Destiny in the first place. There was nothing for her to say, so she quickly turned around and walked out of the nail shop. Ashley felt a burden lift from her at that moment. She no longer had to worry about any confrontations between Carmen and Destiny. They could move on with their lives.

When Ashley and Crystal were done, they prepared to head back after stopping to get something to eat on their way. They took the extra drive and headed to Nancy's downtown. In their opinion, they had the best pizza. They liked it better than Pizza Hut.

After ordering, they sat and talked while waiting for their order. Neither of them knew where this would lead, but the options were definitely open and they both knew that Destiny wouldn't have a problem with having an open relationship.

****

Back at their apartment, Destiny sat on the sofa in silence. There had been so many thoughts running through her mind, so she appreciated this time alone. Shit was crazy right now, but she was happy to see Crystal and Ashley getting along. Most importantly, she had a

DESTINY IS ALL I NEED

chance to hear Crystal's side of everything. Now she understood better. She already knew that Crystal would eventually get tired of sharing her with Ashley. Who didn't want a love of their own? Destiny was never the one to leave loose ends so, in a way, she was glad that Crystal had shown up. Now she was here,and everything had changed.

Would this be beneficial? The possibilities were unlimited but for now, she wouldn't worry about all of that.

Destiny heard keys at the front door and knew it was Ashley and Crystal. Her eyes lit up as she looked at the two of them. They were absolutely beautiful. A smile spread across her lips as she got up to help them with the food and drinks they were carrying.

Chapter 26

All for One

Crystal stayed with Ashley and Destiny for two weeks straight after the day she showed up because they were having so much fun together. The only time she left was to pick up clothes from her apartment. Destiny had finally convinced Ashley to stop messing around with the "powder". They knew it was a part of their past they needed to let go of in order to move forward. Crystal never knew about Ashley messing around with drugs. As long as it was over, neither of them had anything to worry about.

The three of them had a serious talk about what their plans were as far as the "open relationship" went. It seemed that Ashley and Crystal were willing to do whatever it took to make things work. It sounded crazy, but they both wanted Destiny, no matter what. One would think this left no room for balance and stability, but the three of them made it work.

Ashley and Crystal catered to Destiny, and she catered to them in return. When they went out, everybody gave them crazy looks. They even heard some people make snide remarks, but they didn't pay it any attention. They were "one". There was love and understanding between them and they didn't give a fuck how others felt about it. It felt so good to have some kind of order in their lives without drama.

Once Ashley had gotten her head back into her work, she was able to bring Crystal and Destiny in. Everything was working out perfectly.

After working a few months together, the three of them found a bigger place to live. It was right up their alley when they found the three bedroom brick house in Decatur. It wasn't anything fancy, but they were comfortable there. As they prepared to go out shopping for new furniture, they knew that this would be something to remember. The three of them settled on a dark brown leather living room suit. They matched up the rugs and wall pictures perfectly. Because they didn't want to be tacky, they also bought end tables and a huge throw rug for the floor. Crystal already had a dinette set that complemented the rest of the furniture. It took them awhile to get everything together and to go pack Crystal's belongings. Their background checks were completed in a couple of days. They knew everything would be cool, so none of them worried about the results.

On a Friday, Ashley received the call that let them know that they had been approved. She passed the information on to her "girlfriends". What a great way to start the weekend! After finding some guys to help them move, it wasn't long before they were in their new place.

Destiny was still in shock over all that had transpired, but all she could do was smile because now, she had a real reason to.

The End

Part Two Reader's Guide Questions

1. Do you think Ashley made the right decisions at the end?

2. How do you feel about Destiny, Ashley and Crystal being in a relationship together?

3. Would you ever consider a relationship as such?

4. Why do you think Ashley turned to drugs after everything Destiny went through?

5. What was your favorite part of Part Two?

6. Do you see any room for change in the story?

~About the Author~

Ebony Nicole grew up in Atlanta GA but currently reside in Decatur Georgia. Her passion for writing extended from her love for poetry which she has been writing since the age of twelve.

In November 2011 her first book entitled "Let God Forgive Him" (Based on a True Story) was published followed by her second book, "Destiny Is All I Need" in 2012. These were followed by her poetry book "Penetration of a Soulful heart" which was released September, 2013 as well as Ebony Nicole's Encouraging Words.

She has many projects to come and looking forward to networking and meeting new people along the way.

www.ingramcontent.com/pod-product-compliance
Lightning Source LLC
Chambersburg PA
CBHW071307130626
46556CB00004B/1500